a thousand feelings

AN ANTHOLOGY OF STORY NUGGETS BY YOUNG WRITERS

BLUE SQUARE
PUBLISHING

A Thousand Feelings
Published by Blue Square Publishing
Littleton, CO

ISBN: 9798681475644

JUV038000 JUVENILE FICTION / Short Stories

Cover and Interior design by Victoria Wolf

Edited by Shelly Wilhelm

BLUE SQUARE
PUBLISHING

To all young writers—know you can achieve anything.

Contents

Introduction

You are holding the literary dreams of eight talented young authors. *A Thousand Feelings* was written during the summer of 2020, in the middle of a pandemic. It's an anthology full of adventure, humor, horror and fantasy, a wild ride of many imaginations. Be prepared to escape, to laugh, cry and jump out of your chair. You will be shocked by just how good these young authors, ranging from ages 9 to 13, are.

We imagined these kids looking back on summer 2020 when we at My Word Publishing started planning a virtual Tween Summer Camp program. This year has been a time of shutdowns, cancelled school and summer programs, masks and endless screen time for kids. Some parents are working from home. Others have had jobs affected.

Watching the tweens around us, in the twilight of childhood, many going through a time of isolation, we wondered, what could we do to give these kids some positive memories of this summer?

The My Word Publishing team decided to put together an online camp for tween writers via Zoom. Every week, award-winning authors, editors and publishing professionals taught the campers about writing and publishing, everything from showing vs. telling to metaphors and cover design. These writers played games, laughed, shared stories, wrote and created. The result is this anthology, something they can treasure and be proud of, something positive they can remember from this challenging time in history.

We cannot begin to tell you how proud we are of these writers. We have seen their writing evolve. Their creativity, talent and work ethic are outstanding. The quality of team-work, leadership and professionalism were surprising, not just because of the ages involved, but because it was all on Zoom.

The writers came up with the theme for the book, as well as its title, *A Thousand Feelings*. Each story begins with some variation on I had a feeling…

Stories have been edited with a light touch. The revisions have been done by the authors themselves.

It has been a joy to work with these writers each week this summer, and we hope you find joy in reading their work.

—K.B. Jensen, author, publishing consultant and head camp counselor, & Shelly Wilhelm, lead editor, children's publishing consultant and camp counselor

To my family.

—Helena Smith-Donald

The Stop Sign That Was Alive

By
Helena Smith-Donald

walking around town one day, I had a feeling I was being watched. I turned around. I was pretty sure the stop sign on the corner had just been wiggling in the wind but there was definitely no wind.

"It's okay," I said gently. "I won't tell anyone you're alive."

Wait a second. Was I just talking to a stop sign? I asked myself, embarrassed. I decided to forget about it. Then, it moved again.

The sign bent forward and back, as if trying to tell me it was animate. I realized I might not be crazy even though I was still embarrassed by the question I had asked a few seconds ago. *It's just your imagination*, one part of my brain insisted. *That sign just moved!* the other side of my brain said. That side won.

"Can you talk?" I asked. It seemed to glance around. Then it rattled back and forth or maybe shook its head. "That's okay," I said. "We'll just use body language." It nodded up and down.

"So ..." I said, trying to be casual, "are all 'inanimate' objects actually alive? Or just you?" The sign looked confused because I had asked two opposite questions at once. "Just answer the first question," I told it.

It stopped looking confused, paused a moment, then shook its head. "Are you the only one then?" I asked. It nodded and turned its "head" (the sign part, not the pole) away. I wasn't sure, but I thought I saw what looked like a raindrop on it. "I'm sorry," I said. Just then, one of my friends from school walked up.

"Talking to yourself?" she asked. I stopped, startled, and said, "Yeah, I—am." She laughed. "Don't worry. I do it too. Though it's kinda weird to say 'sorry' to yourself. Wait—are you using a phone even though you're not supposed to? I didn't think you had that in you!" She grinned excitedly.

"I don't even have a phone!" I exclaimed. "I, uh, was practicing apologizing to my friend for, um, not bringing the food she traded me for, because I'm, uh, going to change the deal?" I tried to make it seem like something someone normal would be doing.

She didn't seem to buy it, but said, "Okay? Well, see ya!"

I nodded. "Yeah, see ya!" I said, plastering a fake smile onto my face.

Once she was out of sight, I turned back to the sign.

"Phew!" I said, in a quieter voice. "We were almost caught!" I got the sense it felt relieved, then realized the marks on its face were changing!

"I think I may have figured something out! Are those marks your eyes, nose, and eyebrows?" I asked. It nodded.

"And those weird bulges are your ears?" I said, finally figuring it out. It nodded but turned away again. "Oh, sorry!" I exclaimed, before quieting again. "I didn't mean they were weird." It nodded slightly, as if saying, "It's okay."

After thinking a moment, a lightbulb went off. "So that's why you can't talk!" I said. "You have no mouth. But you do have feet or something like them. Can you move?" I asked. It nodded and then shook its head. I thought for a moment before responding.

"Are you stuck in the sidewalk?" I asked. The sign nodded sadly. "Do you want to be free?" I asked. It nodded again. This time it seemed more curious and hopeful. It knew I had a plan. "Do you think I can dig you out?" I asked with a big smile on my face. It nodded excitedly and its eyes lit up. I found a stick, got down on my knees, and started digging.

Ten minutes later, I still wasn't done. It did occur to me that the sign could actually not be alive, and I was either imagining it, or it was wiggling for some other reason. But I quickly pushed away that thought because when you don't want something to be true, you sometimes tell yourself that you're right.

"Hey, at least I should be done soon!" I said and took a short break to catch my breath. The sign nodded, agreeing with me. Five minutes after that, I was *really* tired. "I might give up," I said. "Sorry." I shrugged. What I didn't say was that I was partly giving up because I thought I might have been crazy.

"Maybe another time," I told the sign. It rattled its head vigorously, seeming to say, "Don't give up! You're really close. I can feel it!" I sighed and tried one more time. *It's probably not my imagination*, I told myself.

I could tell it was pushing hard to be free, too, from the way its eyebrow marks were scrunched. Then suddenly it popped right out of the ground. "Whoa!" I exclaimed, jumping back. Then I realized what had just happened.

"Hooray!" I shouted for joy. "I did it!" Then I realized that I may just have randomly dug a stop sign out of the ground and stopped shouting.

The sign's "eyes" smiled and it nodded excitedly. It hopped about recklessly. I did too, then stopped myself before we crashed or someone saw me. For all I knew, its hopping around could have been my imagination. Someone could have walked by and seen me hopping around with a stop sign lying on the sidewalk next to me. I satisfied myself with just grinning really widely.

Once it was tired of hopping everywhere, it flopped down on the ground to rest. Then it looked sad again. "What's wrong, sign?" I asked it. It looked even sadder. "Oh, I get it," I said. "You can't talk, so you can't tell me anything! We'll fix that. Somehow." After a moment, I realized I should call it by its name, not "sign."

"What's your name?" I asked the stop sign. "Oh, right, you can't respond. Does your name sound like 'sign'?" It nodded excitedly. "So it starts with an 's'?" I checked to make sure.

It nodded again. "Hmmmm. Silas?" I asked. It shook its

head in a way that said "obviously not." "Sia?" The sign shook its head again.

"No?" I said. "How about Simon?" It scrunched its eyebrows, thinking. After a few seconds, though, it was nodding its head excitedly. "Simon? Okay, Simon!" I smiled. "I like that, Simon the Sign!" It nodded again. "Got it, Simon," I said.

"Well, you can't talk," I said. "But you *can* see, right? And smell and hear?" Simon the Sign sat up and nodded. It was a peculiar sight, watching a stop sign sit up. He bent in the middle and slowly rose. If somebody else was looking at Simon and nothing else, they might have thought it had been hit in a storm. It looked like he had been attacked! I laughed out loud at the sight.

"So, why?" I asked, wondering about his senses again. He looked confused and tilted his head to the side. I couldn't figure it out, so I started thinking about mine.

"Why can *I* talk, smell, see and hear?" I asked. After a little while, I realized something. "It's because I have a mouth, nose, eyes and ears that *work*!" I exclaimed. Simon nodded excitedly. "And you do too! Except you have no mouth at all." I frowned.

"Why don't you have a mouth?" I asked. Simon tilted his head to the side again. I stroked my chin, thinking, and tried again. "How did you get your ears, eyes, and nose to work? Do you know?" I asked. Simon the Sign thought for a moment then nodded, telling me it remembered. "So, was it at a store?" He shook his head. "Really?" I asked. I had been sure it was going to be in a store.

"Oh. Then ... um ... one second—let me think," I said, thinking. *How else could Simon have gotten them?* "Wait. Was it magic?" Simon the Sign shook his head. Then nodded. Then shook his head again.

"You make no sense," I said. Then after another moment of thought, I asked, "Was it magic that made you alive, but it didn't give you your senses? And your senses worked right away?" I asked. Simon nodded excitedly. "Oh! Did something dent you? Or did someone draw on you?" I exclaimed. The sign started nodding.

"I know!" I exclaimed. "I will draw a mouth on you!" I searched for a pen in my backpack. There wasn't one. "Simon, come with me to the store so I can buy a pencil or pen, okay?" He nodded, then got low to the ground.

"What?" I asked. Simon then proceeded to half-climb on my back. "I can't carry you!" I said. He just nodded and crouched down again. I raised one eyebrow. "What?" I asked again. He pretended to climb on my back again and crouched down once more, pointing at me with his head. "Oh, you want me to go on your back. Okay! Thank you," I said, finally understanding his gestures.

Simon crouched down once more. I gently put one foot on his back, then switched my weight back and forth a few times. I took a deep breath and hoisted myself up. "Wow, you're slippery!" I exclaimed, just barely catching myself.

Simon waited a minute for me to stabilize myself, then stood up fully. "Whoa!" I cried out. Again, I almost fell but managed to stay on. I gripped his head as he began to walk. I held on as tight as I could as we hopped along.

His motions were very jerky. In fact, I almost fell off a bunch of times. But we finally reached the store where I slid off. "I feel a little motion sick," I told Simon. "I'm just going to take a minute to catch my breath." Two minutes later, I had a pencil in my hand. Luckily, nobody questioned why I needed a single pencil or why there was a stop sign in the middle of the sidewalk. I could tell everyone wanted to ask though. I walked out of the store. Quickly, so I wouldn't draw more attention than I already had. I could only hope no one connected me with Simon.

"Alright, you ready?" I asked Simon. He nodded. "Here goes," I said. I drew an open mouth with teeth on him. "Teeth probably help you make certain sounds," I explained. I added a tongue as an afterthought.

"Now say something!" I prompted. Simon took a deep breath, breathing in air for the first time. "Hello," he said. My mouth dropped open. "You can—talk! You can actually talk!" I exclaimed. Simon smiled and said, "Yes! I can talk!" Then it was like that scene in *Charlotte's Web* when Wilbur finds out he can talk.

We started hopping around with me yelling, "You can talk!" and him yelling, "I can talk!" with the same enthusiasm. As people started staring, I pulled him into an alley and hoped nobody realized what had happened.

"I never thought I would have a talking stop sign as a friend!" I exclaimed.

"I never thought I would be able to talk or have a human as a friend!" Simon responded. We both grinned at each other and went back to our celebrations. (Our celebrations included me doing a cartwheel and him trying to do one and falling on his head. It turned out okay though, because he bounced right back up.)

From that day on, Simon the Sign and I were great

friends. I would ride on his back to school and he would wait outside during class. It took a while (three months!) but I finally got used to the jerkiness of his movements. I introduced him to my family, who thought he was a little weird, but I loved him nonetheless. We did everything together through sun and rain, winter and summer; he even attended my birthday party!

College was a tougher obstacle, because Simon didn't want me to forget him. We finally settled on him staying home and using my mom to keep in contact. Apparently, my mom was his official scribe for letters and it was a tough job.

Simon would start talking and talking as my mom struggled to write it all down. Then he would impatiently say, "Did you catch that? The part about this and the part about that? Don't forget this part," and things like that. But it couldn't have been *that* bad.

Simon the Sign stayed with me my whole life. He may have been quirky, but he was my best friend. We lived happily ever after.

Helena Smith-Donald is a reader, writer, soccer player, musician and artist, and is entering sixth grade. She is interested in becoming a teacher one day. She loves animals and nature. She started writing at age five. Helena lives in Chicago, Illinois, with her parents, her brother and her sister.

I'd like to thank my family, because if I don't, I'll get in trouble. LOL.

—Monte Canales

Dart Wars

By
Monte Canales

I have a feeling that today is going to be a tough day, but I ignore it. It starts as a normal day. I get up slowly, put my clothes on and go eat breakfast. Cinnamon Toast Crunch is my favorite cereal. I sit there on the recliner couch eating my cereal and watching *Star Wars Rebels* when my phone rings. It is a call from Jack, the team leader of our dart war team. I let it go to voicemail because my hands are covered in cinnamon sugar.

"Hey, Monte, we are getting the team together at my house to raid an enemy's supply outpost later. Wanna come?"

You see, we have a competition every year against the rich kids across town. Our game is like Capture the Flag and Dodgeball put together. The rules are simple. If you get shot by a dart, you are out. If your team leader gets captured or shot, the game is over. Pretty simple, right? Wrong! You can do almost anything you like in this competition. Attack, hide, ambush, camp outside an enemy base or raid an enemy base. Even shoot an enemy on the way to or from school. You can use custom guns for longer range and harder shots too. What I'm saying is, it's like living in a video game. It is so cool! Oh, and you can't shoot a player while they are sleeping in their bed. That's about the only thing you can't do.

I am all in! I get my yellow Fortnite gun and my light blue plastic container shield and slowly creep out the door. I look left, right, and left again. Not only for cars but for enemies that could be camping on my doorstep. The coast is clear. I run to Jack's house as fast as a rocket. I hold my shield nervously. I'm afraid that someone could sneak up and shoot me in the back. One minute later I am at his house. The team is already there.

"Monte!" a voice calls to me. It is my best friend, Patrick. He is wearing the face shield his mom gave him last Christmas.

"Pat! Good to see you! How'd you sleep?"

"Lying down," he chuckles. I shake my head and chuckle too.

Jack comes down from his room with the board game Risk. He takes out some soldiers and a cannon piece and puts them on the table.

"Okay, guys, here's the plan," Jack says as he places the pieces on a hand-drawn map of our neighborhood.

"The blue squadron will sneak around the back of the house while the red squadron will rush the front of the house." He moves the four blue pieces to the back of the house on the board and the four reds to the front of the house.

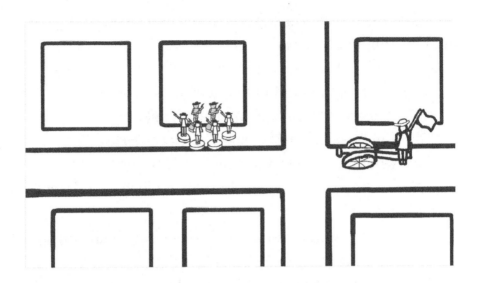

"We will take out the guards here and here." He continues placing four gray soldiers on the board.

"After that, the blue squad will go to the basement to see if they can find more ammunition, and the red squad will check the main floor for any soldiers or ammunition. After we are finished with our mission, we will meet back at the minivan. Or as I like to call it, the 'AV.' Short for armored van." He puts a cannon piece on the road.

"Does anyone need to hear the plan again?" No one answers. "Does anyone have any questions?" Several hands rise. "Of course, you do!"

Most of the questions are about ammunition and how much time we have for the mission. Also what type of weapons they will be carrying and so on. They are answered with a, "We'll find out when we get there," from Jack.

"You know I like my briefings brief, so get your ammunition and guns all sorted out. We are leaving at 11:30 a.m. MOVE, MOVE, MOVE!"

I walk up to Jack. "Jack, I know that you're smart at planning and all, but there are eight of us and who knows how many of them," I say nervously.

"So?" Jack replies without concern.

"So ... do you have a backup plan?" I ask.

"We don't need a backup plan," Jack remarks.

"But what if we get trapped or, or," I stutter.

"We don't need one. I have this plan foolproof," Jack says with confidence.

"Okay, but if we get captured, I'm blaming it all on you," I say with a smirk.

At 11:30 a.m. everyone piles into the AV. Jack's mom is the getaway driver. She's always looking out for us. We park a block away from the supply outpost house. Our main base is five blocks away.

The first battle we had in the rich neighborhood, I thought I'd see hedge clippings of horsemen, giant fountains, Olympic-sized swimming pools and humongous mansions. But I was pretty disappointed because it looked almost exactly like our neighborhood with a few more pools and security cameras. The cars, though, they were different. Corvettes, convertibles and a sparkling green titanium-looking car. They looked rich.

We get out of the AV and crouch behind white fences, shimmy under fancy cars and hide behind trash cans and discarded Amazon boxes. There we are, just across the street from their supply outpost. Jack is right. There are only two guards at the front of the house and according to the blue squad on our walkie-talkies, there are two guards at the back as well. Before the mission started, Jack gave each squad a walkie-talkie just in case we got separated. They are really, really good. They are probably a gift from his grandmom for his birthday. She always spoils him.

The blue squadron is already climbing over the fence on the left side of the house and dropping into the bushes. Surprisingly quietly too. They pause.

The two guards at the front are wearing face shields just like Patrick. Jack whispers the GO code to rush the front and back doors. As I shoot one of the guards in the face, Patrick shoots down the other. Before we rush in, we load up our guns. Jack pretends to kick open the door, and right as he does, we hear something smash behind the door. Jack knocked the wind out of a kid. I thought this only happens in cartoons but apparently it happens in real life too.

We shoot him right when we see him. I give a little giggle and so does Patrick because it is pretty funny. Before we look for supplies, we secure the inside looking for anyone else. As I come into the kitchen, I see a dart fly and hit some kid right in the forehead. It shocks me. He is wearing a beanie and eating a cookie standing next to the cookie jar. As he drops like a rag doll to the floor, he takes the cookie out of his mouth, but as he hits the ground, he continues eating.

"Who did that?" Patrick asks.

"Was it Molly? asks Jason, a red squad member who wants to be cool but isn't.

"It couldn't be," I say. Just then a different kid comes around the corner with face paint on. We all have our guns ready except Jack. He has cat-like reflexes. We know this person.

So before I tell you who it is, let me tell you something else about the game. There is a third party in this competition.

The Neutrals. Or some people call them The Switzerlands. They aren't on any team. They help both sides ... for a price. The most common payment is king-size candy bars or boxes of cereal. And the most wanted payment is money. Cold. Hard. Cash.

"Whoa! Clayton!" Jack says surprisingly to his best friend. "It's you?"

"Long time no see," Clayton says coolly.

"Nice shot!" Jack exclaims.

"Head shot," Clayton boasts.

Jack and Clayton have a looong conversation. I'd say too long. We collect all the ammunition in about 15 minutes, but we stay there even longer because those two are still chatting. It is like the dart war isn't even going on! After a few minutes we get bored and Patrick takes out his bag of cards and candy. We all do the same thing minus the cards. Another five minutes go by and eventually we play Rock, Paper, Scissors to find out who should go tell Jack that it's time to go. FYI—I throw rock and the other two throw paper. *How does paper beat rock anyway?* I think to myself.

I slowly walk up behind Jack to whisper that we have to go. He moans and whines and finally we get out of the outpost with all the ammo and weapons. Clayton comes with us.

While Jack's mom drives back to home base, we get ambushed by two rich kids with guns blazing! They put tacks on the road to pop out our tires and prevent us from getting back to safety too. Their tactics worked multiple times before but after the last attack, we put a plow on the front of the van constructed out of duct tape, cardboard and Flex Seal so the "tack-tic" is useless.

"Who are they?" shouts Clayton.

"No time to explain. I'll tell you at home base," blurts Jack. As they continue firing, one of us hits one of them and they drop to the hot asphalt behind us. We keep firing while the last kid chases us for another block and collapses to the ground.

Jack's mom shouts, "Hey, if my tires pop, it's coming out of your allowances!" as she plows through several more waves of poppers and tacks like a bulldozer.

At base camp we get out of the car so fast it's as if we all have to go to the bathroom.

"I'm going to the store. Do you boys need anything?" calls Jack's mom.

"NoMomthanksgoodbye!" Jack says in one breath as he closes the house door behind him. He wedges a chair under the handle. We flick on the lights and close the windows while Jack also pushes a box mounted on the wall.

"Lockdown complete," it sounds.

"To your battle stations!" Jack shouts like an Army commander.

Patrick and I run up the stairs with the rest of the blue squadron and are horrified by what we see when we look out the window.

"Oh no!" We both yell in unison. Tons of rich kids are marching toward us with heavy guns, snipers and even dual pistols. Patrick and I both grab our own guns, but we know we are outnumbered and outgunned. Patrick quickly snaps a picture of the entourage of kids coming our way and hits send.

Patrick texts someone on his phone. As he does, they

start to open fire on us. The bullets barely miss us. Many fly inside the base because the windows are still open upstairs; some hit the blue squadron. We quickly close the windows. We hear pounding on the door downstairs. Patrick gets another text. This time it's from Jack. I don't know what it says but from the look on Patrick's face, it seems urgent.

Suddenly, a loud bang fills the house. Then silence for a few seconds. We hear marching into the house. We peek out the window. The rich kids are coming INSIDE our base. I am astonished how many kids there are. I am nervous they may come up and shoot us too.

Patrick whispers, "Monte, how 'bout we throw the mattress out the side window and jump, then ambush them from the front?"

I nod. We shove the mattress out the window. I'm pretty scared at first, but I get the guts up and jump out the window. It isn't that bad. He has a Purple mattress and it is pretty soft actually. Before Patrick jumps out the window, he throws down a blue dart shotgun. Patrick and I creep to the front door and find out that the front door is gone. I mean totally knocked in.

I see the person that's on top of the fallen door is none other than the rich kids team leader, Pierce Carlston. Seeing Pierce, I whisper to Patrick, "Do you have any ammo in that shotgun?

He says, "One round. Why?"

Patrick hands me the shotgun and says, "I see where you are going with this."

I walk up behind him, "Hey!" I yell. Pierce turns around and I immediately shoot him with the last round. There is silence for a few seconds, then I say, smugly looking at Jack, "Now that's a backup plan!"

I motion to everyone, "Well, what are you waiting for? An invitation?" The rest of the blue squad yells from upstairs, "Yahoo!!" "Right on!" "We did it!!" The only person left upstairs on the red squad exclaims, "Woo-hoo! Take that, rich kids!"

I look around and see that Jack's mom is coming back from the grocery store with two bags in her hands. "Oh no. Our victory didn't last that long," I moan, looking around at the messy room.

"Oh GREAT," Jack whines. "My mom is going to KILL me! Quick, hide me!" he exclaims as he jumps into a pile of pillows in the corner.

Everyone bursts into laughter. Even the rich kids.

Monte Canales is an author, artist, gamer and sixth-grader. He is interested in becoming a graphic novelist and YouTuber one day. Monte loves his family, his friends, spaghetti and video games. He started writing and creating comics at age 8. Monte lives in Denver, Colorado, with his mom, dad and two lazy fish named Magic Carp and Gyarados.

*To my second-grade teacher, she
inspired me to read, write and learn. And to my
best friend, for always being by my side.*

—Riley Meissner

Mary Lynn's Freak School

By
Riley Meissner

I had an anxious feeling. My mom and dad were sending me off to boarding school. There wasn't really a reason. "It will build character," Dad had said. I had a new school, new friends, and possibly new bullies to look forward to. And on top of that, a six-hour cab drive to the school. So, after packing my bags and saying my goodbyes, I was off to boarding school.

The school sign was a curious one. "Mary Lynn's Primary School for Misbehaving Girls." I snorted and laughed. *My parents could not have sent me here. Right?* I heard footsteps behind me. I stopped and turned around. Shocked, I took a step back. It was two identical twins. They had long, jet black hair and pale skin, and they were wearing short pink dresses with a patch sewn on the side, with lace embroidered everywhere. Their hair curled out at the ends, with pink bows on top of their heads.

"Hi," they said at the same time. "You must be Becky. The new student."

I said nothing.

"Don't be shy," they said.

I thought that only in movies twins spoke in unison.

"I'm not shy. I'm scared," I said turning around. To my surprise, there were two girls behind me. They were identical twins too. They had short strawberry blonde hair and big blue eyes. They wore the same school uniforms as the other girls.

"Hi. I'm Penny, and this is my twin, Jennie," said the one on the left. "And *we* are supposed to show you around," Jennie said, looking at the other twins. "You girls can stop scaring her and scram!" Jennie added. The first set of twins turned around and quickly left without looking back. They must have really been scared of her or something.

"Thanks, guys. They were really starting to freak me out," I said.

"Oh well, you'd better get used to it," Penny warned me.

"Why?" I asked unknowingly.

"Everyone here has a twin. Except you. Here's your uniform. You are sharing dorm C with us. Okay, see you in class," Jenny said, ushering me toward a building with a large C on the door on the far side of the dirt-covered grounds. I followed with the uniform in my hands.

After changing, I realized that I was going to be miserable. The grounds were hazy, my uniform was SUPER itchy, and I worried that I would be lonely since I was the only one without a twin. I spent most of the day hiding out in the library. I was excited to see that the fantasy section was large, and there was a stray book about fairies in the realistic fiction section. I pulled it down. Nothing happened. I shrugged. It was worth a shot to see if some bookcase would open or something. I put the book back on the shelf. I thought I heard something from behind me. I spun around and jumped 10 feet in the air. It was the strange twins from earlier.

"I'm Willow, and this is my twin, Sookie," said the one on the right.

"Yeah, don't be scared. We just wanna play. We have been looking for you for hours," said Willow.

"Alright. Well, nice meeting you, I just gotta go over there to uh," my mind blanked. "Talk to," again, I had no excuse. "The janitor. I love cleaning."

"He quit last night. At 3 a.m.," said Sookie.

"You should know only bad things happen at 3 a.m.," added Willow.

"He ran out into the street. It didn't end well," Sookie said.

"HE DIED?" I yelled.

"No. Just broke his leg." Willow laughed. "My, my what a negative Nancy you are."

"Yes, Regan and Monica will love meeting her," Sookie said.

"Okay, I'll see you outside your dorm room in ten minutes, guys," I said. When I was alone, I sprinted for my dorm. I found Jennie and Penny inside the lobby and hurriedly locked the door. "Who are Regan and Monica?" I demanded.

They looked at each other for a long time before Jennie said, "They were two strange girls; they ran into the woods on the edge of the school grounds. The next week, everyone finally realized they were missing. After about a month, students began saying they saw them coming out of the woods every night. They would pull their hair or mock them in their sleep. Finally, their bodies were found in the woods. They had eaten poison berries, and the red juice was dripping down their faces. Legend has it they still haunt the school grounds."

"Their younger sisters, Willow and Sookie, say they still have tea parties and dance lessons with their sisters," Penny added. "They even said they played with a Ouija board with Regan and Monica."

I panicked and looked blankly at them. "I told them I would meet them outside their dorm room in ten minutes. That was fifteen minutes ago," I said.

"Ooh. You're late. Spooky," Jennie mocked.

"Hey, let her finish!" Penny said.

"I said I would meet them there five minutes ago to meet Regan and Monica." I said, worried. Blankly, the twins stared at me. Just then, we heard a banging on the door. The doorknob rattled as the girls tried to open it.

"Becky, you're late!" they yelled. I couldn't tell which one, because even their voices were identical.

"Um, she isn't here," Penny yelled.

"Yeah, Penny and I are just reading and doing homework in here," Jennie added.

"She isn't here?" one of the twins asked.

"Um, yeah," Jennie said, pushing me under the bed.

Penny opened the door. The girls looked around, my heart racing. "Fine. She isn't here. But if she is, you have to tell us. We are worried that she might be hurt," said a twin. That night, I knew I had to escape. I grabbed my bags and headed for the forest. There, I saw the girls. They looked happy to see me. "It's late. Shouldn't you be in bed?" one asked.

"Yes. There might be scary things in the woods late at night," said the other.

"Okay, Willow, Regan. I'm sorry that I didn't meet you guys, I thought you were in dorm B. Anyway, I need to leave." I saw another set of Regan and Willow come out from behind them.

"Want to play a game?" asked one.

"Hide and seek," another added.

"Sure, it will be fun," said a third.

"Come on, Becky. You know it will be fun," said the last.

"Okay," I said. "I'll seek."

"No. You hide; the four of us will seek," said one in the middle.

"We will count to 10. Ready? 10, 9 … ." I ran as fast as I could back to the dorm. It has been four years, and I haven't seen any of the girls since that night.

I had convinced my parents to move out of state.

Riley Meissner is a devoted author, who has loved writing since she was seven. Riley wants to be a horror author when she grows up. She likes spending time outside with friends and family, doing things such as camping and bike riding. Riley lives in Littleton, Colorado, and is going into sixth grade. What inspires Riley is her love of books. Riley also loves to paint and has hosted two art shows, donating the money to a cat shelter. Riley hopes to accomplish more things to help other people and animals.

*Thank you to my family for supporting me and
my friends who I let read my first draft.*

—Ellyse Brumfield

Phoenix Feathers

By
Ellyse Brumfield

Luelle had the strange feeling she was being watched. She was on her way to her best friend Alec's house in the middle of nowhere surrounded by forest just like hers. Luelle looked around. At first she saw nothing out of the ordinary: Tall pine trees and twigs littered the ground; bushes and poison oak lay on the forest floor like a blanket. Then she saw it. A huge centipede the size of a semitruck was crouched behind a pine; the tree did nothing to conceal it though.

Luelle stepped back. She was really starting to hate centipedes. It seemed wherever she went, there was a giant mutant bug or some sort of monster, but no one else ever saw the things or believed Luelle when she told them about the monsters. She stepped back again—once, twice, three times—before her foot found and snapped a twig. The arthropod's head, if you could call it a head, snapped up. All 177 pairs of legs charged her. Luelle fell back, scrambling up a tree as fast as she could. The centipede, having poor eyesight, didn't know where she had gone. It skittered around, its feelers pressed to the floor.

It's now or never, Luelle thought. *One … two … three!* She leaped down from her tree branch and onto another one lower down. She reached out to another branch connected to the tree next to hers. She wasn't sure if it would hold her weight, but she had to try. She took a deep breath and jumped, swinging from the branch and landing on another right next to it; the branch bent from her weight. Luelle tried to leap to the next branch, but the branch under her had already snapped.

By this time, the centipede had located where Luelle was. It had run halfway up her tree, the pine leaning to the left slightly from the massive bug, when she fell. Luelle fell in slow motion. Looking back on it, Luelle would have liked to say she had laughed in the face of death, thought of a brave plan quickly and acted it out, but all that came out of Luelle's mouth was, "AHHH!"

And then, out of nowhere, just as Luelle was about to fall and break every bone in her body and/or get eaten by a giant arthropod, a flash of gold and red tackled her out of midair. Luelle felt as if her stomach had been left over by the broken tree branch. She was about to stand up, when she realized she was still in the air, the treetops dangling beneath her feet. Luelle noticed she was still screaming and closed her mouth at once. She looked up and saw that the hood of her sweatshirt was grasped by huge gray talons.

Luelle looked up higher and almost screamed again—a huge red and gold bird was carrying her. It must have had a wingspan of 10 to 15 feet; it had a long, sharp beak that looked like it was made of solid gold. Luelle wanted to yell something at the bird like, "Hey! Put me down!" or "Who are you?" but realized there was no point in doing that because it was a bird. She also didn't think struggling was a good idea, as she would probably end up plummeting to her death. So she stayed where she was and was silent.

You might be wondering why Luelle seemed so chill about this, but that's because she was used to weird things happening to her. After a few minutes, the strange bird creature landed on a small cliff that Luelle didn't even know existed. As far as she was concerned, there weren't any mountains like that in Rangeley, Maine, or at least not the part that she lived in.

The bird dropped her in a heap on the stony ground. Luelle stood up and brushed herself off as the golden bird flew into a cave. She realized the bird gave off a faint yellowish glow. Thirty seconds later, a figure in a black cloak stepped out of the cave. The huge bird had shrunk to the size of an Andean condor and was perched precariously on his shoulder.

"W-who are you?" Luelle asked, stepping back a couple of steps.

"I am Gethin," the person said, lowering their hood. They had short, dark brown hair beginning to gray. The man looked like he was in his early fifties or sixties.

"T-that doesn't r-really answer my question," Luelle managed, "and also, why i-is there a giant bird on your sh-shoulder?"

"To answer your second question, this is Ember—" The bird squawked, interrupting Gethin who rolled his grayish eyes in annoyance. "I mean Fawkes. He insists that EVERY-ONE call him Fawkes ever since he read *Harry Potter*. He's a phoenix by the way."

"U-um that thing, phoenix," Luelle said quickly, "can read?" She didn't know what was weirder, that phoenixes where supposedly real or that they could read—definitely the latter.

"Of course, he can read!" Gethin said, like that was the most obvious thing in the world. "He's over 600 years old. You think he wouldn't open a book after a while?"

"O-oh." Luelle was pretty sure that if Fawkes tried to open a book, he would shred it into confetti, but she kept her mouth shut.

"Anyway, I sent Emb-Fawkes," Gethin looked meaningfully at the phoenix, "after you as soon as I could, and it's a good thing I did too. Fawkes said that you were in the middle of falling to your death and being eaten by an ingens scolopendra."

"I'm sorry, an engine's scallop—what?" Luelle asked, taking another step backward.

"Ingens scolopendra. It literally means huge centipede in Latin."

"Wait y-you see them too? Th-the monsters, the huge bugs, everything!"

"Of course, I see them, only obliviouses can't," Gethin replied.

"What's an oblivious?" Luelle asked.

"The opposite of an aware, which is someone or

something that can see the real world behind the veil—"

"Veil?"

"Yes, the thing that separates the magical world from the so-called normal world. It stops most humans from seeing what is real and what is not, like how someone might see Fawkes and think he's a raven or a blackbird."

"Oookay? Go on then." Luelle didn't know what else to say.

"So what I was saying was an example of an aware would be you, I or your friend Alec the shapeshifter—"

"SHAPESHIFTER!?" Luelle took another step backward and almost fell off the cliff. As she stumbled, falling backward, Gethin grabbed her hand and pulled her up to safety.

"Yes, as I was saying before you tried to fall to your death for the second time in about half an hour, Alec is a shapeshifter. Well, she doesn't know yet but that's not the point—"

"How do you know?" Luelle interrupted. "So far, you sound like some crazy stalker, and I'm supposed to trust you!?" Luelle snatched her arm away from Gethin, lowering herself to the ground, looking for a hand or foothold to start her descent down.

"And … what do you think you're doing?" Gethin asked.

"I'm leaving. I'm gonna climb down and go to Alec's house and act like this never happened."

"No …" Gethin said. "You're going to *try* to climb down, fall, then end up breaking your neck and probably every bone in your body." Luelle glared at him. "Or I could have Fawkes bring you down safely, but if I have him do that, then you have to listen to the rest of what I have to say."

"Fine, deal then," Luelle said, shaking Gethin's hand.

"Now that we have that sorted out, I think we need to talk to Alec." Gethin snapped his fingers, and Luelle's best friend, Alec, appeared in a flurry of purplish smoke.

"What the—!?" Alec began, looking around herself. "How did I—"

"Don't worry, Alecksandria, you'll be fine. I just teleported you here for a few minutes," Gethin said.

"Who are you? And how do you know my name!?" Alec asked, stepping back a little, her short, wavy black hair blowing in the wind. "Luelle? What are you doing here?"

"No idea. As far as I'm concerned, this is just one big hallucination," Luelle replied, trying not to look as terrified as she felt. *How did Gethin do that?*

"Okay, be quiet. Time is short, and we need to make sure that no one notices Alec is missing before I teleport her back, so I'm just gonna explain this the short way," Gethin said. "Alec, you are a shapeshifter and your friend is a monster fighter."

There was silence for a few moments before the girls both yelled, "WHAT!?"

"The prophecies foretold that a shapeshifter and monster fighter would one day save the world, and that day is probably this week, so I'm supposed to train you guys to fight monsters and stuff so we can all avoid Armageddon, Ragnarok, the apocalypse, the end of the world as we know it, whatever you want to call it—it all means the same thing."

"And we know this is real because …?" Alec asked.

"Did you not just get teleported to a cliff top?" Gethin asked.

"Okay, good point," Alec said. Luelle had no idea what the heck was happening, so she decided to just go with it because the sooner this was over the better.

"So anyway, that means it's my duty to give you this." Gethin pulled out a long, thin metal cylinder from the folds of his robes and handed it to Alec.

"A metal stick, thanks ..." Alec said sarcastically.

"It is not a stick, it's a staff, and for Luelle—" Gethin made an odd whistling noise to Ember, or Fawkes or whatever his name was. He took off from Gethin's shoulder and flew into the cave behind Gethin, who stood there patiently for a few minutes until Fawkes came back, carrying a long package wrapped in brown paper.

He dropped it at Luelle's feet. Luelle bent to open it. As she unwrapped the paper, a dark, polished, wooden bow fell out, as well as a leather quiver and a dozen smooth arrows, flecked with red and gold feathers that looked like they had once belonged to Fawkes.

"Okay ... what am I supposed to do with—" Luelle started, but was cut off by a noise so loud, the earth shook. A huge wolf-like creature that had apparently been silently somehow making its way up the cliff, jumped onto the rocky platform. It howled another time, and Luelle was pretty sure she was about to go deaf if it howled again.

"Well, you can defeat that with it," Gethin yelled over the noise.

"What!? How am I supposed to—"

"Alec can help too. This can be your first training session!" And with that, he and Fawkes disappeared in a puff of smoke.

"Okay, I guess we can try; either way, it's not a good situation to be in," Alec said, looking up at the huge wolf that was the size of an elephant.

"Alright then," Luelle said, struggling to nock an arrow in her bow. She took aim and ... missed. *Oh well, at least I tried,* she thought sarcastically. As the wolf got ready to pounce on Luelle, Alec surprised even herself by turning into a huge puma. She sprung on the wolf, knocking it aside, giving Luelle time to nock another arrow and fire; this time, the arrow hit its target.

Alec leapt off the wolf, turning back into human form and just in time too, because the monster erupted in a blaze of silver flames, leaving nothing but ash behind. Luelle and her friend stood there for a minute or two, staring in silence at where the monster had been until Gethin and Fawkes appeared again in a flurry of smoke.

"Well done!" he said. "That was fast."

"What do we do now?" Luelle asked.

"Now, I train you to fight monsters!" Gethin said enthusiastically.

Ellyse Brumfield is an author, artist, volleyball player, basketball player, horseback rider and sixth-grader. She is interested in becoming a writer or artist one day. She loves drawing and animals, especially horses and cats. She started writing in kindergarten. Ellyse lives in Chicago, Illinois, with her parents, brother and two cats named Sugar and Cocoa.

To all the people who think being different is bad. It's not. Told ya.

—Anika Srinivasan

Jessica Lee Parker

By
Anika Srinivasan

She had a feeling. An eerie feeling, an ominous feeling, a feeling of absolute dread. Jessica Lee Parker, an investigative journalist for a newspaper in the small town of Gillaway, Illinois, was on her way to work when she heard the announcement on the radio.

"Everybody knows about the strange occurrences happening at Gillaway, but this sure is freaky. Adding onto the disappearances and murders, Marie Clinton, a beloved book writer, has mysteriously vanished. We think that she has been kidnapped for her fame, but no one knows what happened. If you have had any sightings of Marie or clues to her disappearance, please call us at 1-800-719-3784."

Jessica smiled. When she and Marie were young, she had told Jessica about how she hated this town and wanted to run away. Jessica had always supported Marie and wanted to do the same, but when she got this job, she realized that she would like to stay in the boring old town.

"Good luck, Marie," Jessica whispered, hoping Marie knew that she was with her in spirit. As Jessica drove closer to the newspaper office, she decided to stop by Marie's house. She had about an hour still before work anyway. Jessica usually got breakfast on her way to work and ate it in her car. When she got to the house about ten minutes later, excitement was bubbling up inside of her.

Marie had a large house, since she had a lot of money. Jessica knew that Marie would leave a note addressed to her, stating that she had run away. Marie had always said she would do that. The door to her house was unlocked, so Jessica opened the door cautiously and slowly peeked around the door. The house was a total mess. Vases and other antique decorations were knocked over. Some were completely shattered. Tables and chairs were missing legs and leaning to the side. Different things from all over littered the floor. Jessica hesitantly stepped inside.

Marie couldn't have made this mess. She's a very neat and tidy person, she thought to herself. Jessica had been to Marie's house many times and knew about the secret cabinet Marie had frequently said she would put her letter in. She crept to the master bedroom and tried opening the door. It was locked. Jessica pushed the thought out of her mind that maybe Marie hadn't run away. It did make sense—the mess downstairs and the locked door.

Jessica rattled the doorknob, and sure enough it came out. Jessica pushed the door open and stepped in. The bedroom was the messiest room in the house. Not only was it more torn apart, but the secret cabinet was empty. The note that Jessica expected was not there! The window was open and the room was drafty. Jessica hurried over. The room was the highest in the house. There was no way that Marie could have jumped.

She was about to go back when she noticed something strange. The paint on the windowsill was slightly chipped, like someone had attached a ladder to it, allowing them to climb down. She took a deep breath and walked out of the room and to her car. On the way to her office, the visit to Marie's house was the only thing that Jessica could think about. She even missed the turn and had to go back because of it.

When Jessica finally arrived at her office, she was bombarded by her boss. "Jessica, you are thirty minutes late. Do you have an explanation?" Her boss, a large man named Nathaniel Dill, put his hand on his hips waiting. Jessica opened her mouth but no words came out. "Yes?" Nathaniel waited.

Jessica took a deep breath and started talking. "When I heard about the missing girl, Marie, I went to her house to see if I could find any clues to her disappearance, since we are friends, or were friends. I found something, although I may need to do more digging." Jessica was surprised that she didn't stutter at all when she spoke. She usually was a nervous mess while talking to other people who had more importance than herself, but she felt different that day.

"Well, in that case, you may go back and figure out what happened. If you don't, you are fired." Nathaniel slammed his fist on the small table next to them. Fear entered Jessica's body. She knew that Nathaniel had some connections to the mayor, and if he fired her, she would never recover. She had no time to waste.

Jessica professionally walked out to her car. She got into the car and turned the keys and the engine started, but a horrible feeling entered her stomach. It was almost nine o'clock in the morning when Jessica got back to Marie's house. Instead of slowly cracking open the door like she had before, she forcefully swung it open and opened her mouth in utter disbelief. She felt sick to her stomach.

The house was entirely clean and tidy, like it was usually. At first, Jessica thought that she had imagined it being a mess earlier, but she rejected that when she found a piece of a broken vase on the floor. She hurried up the stairs to the neat bedroom and opened the secret cupboard. Inside she found a note stating:

Hello, Jessica. I thought that you might look for this note. I did run away. You/Jessica might think I/Marie was kidnapped by someone/something, but no. I have run away. I'll miss you.

The note was strangely short. Jessica furrowed her eyebrows as she read it again. It would have been normal, if not for the slashes in the middle, which stood out boldly. It was very unnerving. Her jaw dropped. It was Morse code. When she was little, her father had taught her one thing in Morse code: SOS, which was three short, three long, and three short. Jessica also knew that it would be ... /// ...written. Marie had been signaling in Morse code for help.

Jessica was about to go look for more clues, but when she turned around, a man was standing there. He put his gloved hand over her mouth while the other held a knife against her throat. He wore a mask that covered his face. The person put the knife in a holder on their waist and pulled out a bottle of pills. Then they opened their fingers a tiny bit and slipped one into Jessica's mouth. Nothing happened at first, but soon after, Jessica lost consciousness and fell to the floor.

When she woke up, she was in a dark room with no windows or doors. The paint on the walls was peeled beyond recognition and the floor had holes in it. Her eyes focused more; she could feel that she had been placed in a chair and tied up. The ropes dug into her skin and left a burning sensation. There was another chair behind her that held another girl, with blonde hair, which contrasted against Jessica's brown hair.

"Hi Jess." The voice sounded very familiar, like an old friend.

"Marie! How did you get here?" Jessica asked.

"Well, I was going to the bathroom and then this guy appeared! Next thing I know I'm strapped to a chair in a dark room!" Marie laughed. Jessica was still confused.

"Marie, we are trapped in a room with no exit, or entrance … . How did we even get in here?" Jessica looked around to see if there was a place they could get out. Marie laughed again as Jessica chuckled. "How did we get in here though?"

"I have no idea at all!" Marie shouted.

"Maybe he built the room around us!" Jessica yelled. For the next hour, they laughed hysterically thinking of how they got in the room. After their throats had become very sore and they couldn't breathe, the girls started to quiet down. Jessica felt tired so she fell asleep in the chair that she was tied to.

"Hey, Jessica cut yourself free with this." Marie slipped

a small pocket knife to her, waking her up. Jessica cut the ropes around her hands and then her stomach. Her legs were numb so when she tried to stand up, she almost fell. Marie chuckled and Jessica smiled. They must have been on some sort of drug that had made them laugh.

"Okay, well we might not be strapped to the chair, but we still are trapped with no way out." Marie had ditched her normal, optimistic self for a downer. Jessica slumped a little and sat in Marie's old chair.

"Wait. Marie, do you see that?" Jessica raised her head and pointed at the wall. Marie walked over and her jaw dropped.

"Is that a …" Marie reached out to the wall.

"Button," Jessica finished. The button was the same color as the wall and was only visible from a certain angle.

"Do you think that it would lead us out?" Marie asked, feeling the smooth surface of the button.

"We can't be sure," Jessica decided. "We should get some sleep,"

"Good thinking. I am tired," Marie sighed and lay on the ground. Jessica did the same, but she had trouble falling asleep. She was terrified and deep down doubted that she would ever make it out alive. Her stomach rumbled.

They slept well that night. When they woke up, though, they were in for a shock. When Jessica woke up, she felt full of energy again, although her mouth was terribly dry and her pants were wet.

"A nice rest was all that I need—oh, you have got to be kidding me." When she looked down, she felt ropes encasing her once again. She shook Marie and got her to wake up. When Marie saw the ropes, she swore and tried to shake them free. "Marie, that won't work, but we can use your knife, right?" Jessica asked. Marie reached her hand in her pocket, but obviously felt nothing.

"They must've taken it when he strapped us to the chair," she stated. Jessica sighed.

"Wait, we could scoot over to the button." Jessica poked Marie's back.

"Okay, let's try it," Marie said.

It was difficult for them to move the chairs in perfect unison without tipping over. A while later, they realized they had been trying for thirty minutes and had gotten about half a foot closer to the button.

"Maybe there is another way." Jessica knew that scooting was their best bet, but it would take hours.

"I don't think so," Marie replied. Jessica sighed and motioned to Marie, telling her to keep moving. Every once in a while, the chair would tip slightly, and they would almost fall over or have a heart attack. It took a very long time for them to get to the button.

"Well, we are here; we are free." Jessica excitedly bounced in the chair and managed to stretch the ropes just enough to loosen them and squeeze through. Marie followed. Jessica took a deep breath and pushed the button. Nothing happened.

"Marie, the door didn't open. Nothing happened!" Jessica shouted.

"Jess, we have a problem." Marie seemed scared.

"I'll say. We are stuck in here and the door didn't open!" Jessica groped the walls for a door frame.

"Jessica, listen to me! Look!" Marie pulled Jessica's shoulders and made her turn around.

"This can't be happening!" Jessica screamed. "No! No!" Gigantic steel spikes emerged from the slowly moving walls. The room got more and more compressed. Jessica and Marie held onto each other. They knew it would be the last time ever.

Anika Srinivasan has been passionate
about writing since she was five years old. She
is an artist and sixth-grader, and she aspires
to become a marine biologist one day. Anika
loves playing guitar and video games, as well as
watching Marvel movies and *Stranger Things*.
Anika lives in Littleton, Colorado, with her
wonderful family and dogs.

To my family, who has always supported me throughout the years.

—Christie D.

Forgiveness

By
Christie D.

He had the feeling. The feeling before it all fell apart. The silence before the incident. The moment when his mom left his life.

CRASH! Liam's mother had jumped in front of him before the car hit his side. The impact came as a jolt. As soon as the collision started, it ended. Still. The car door flung open and Liam ran out, his mother in his arms. He begged her not to go, all the water in his body was streaming from his eyes. Her soft hand reached up to his face as she said, "Take care of your sister. Tell her you love her every day." Liam sadly agreed as he tried to keep his mother alive until the doctors could help. He shook her and cried as he watched the life in her eyes slowly disappear. Her body went limp.

He sobbed like never before while the realization that she was gone washed over him. He sat there for what felt like forever, her body still lying in his arms. When the ambulance came, he fought his hardest to get back to what remained of the woman who had taken care of him and loved him all his life. He screamed with anger and cried with sadness while he struggled to go back to before the crash. As he struggled to go back and change it all. As he struggled to have his mother alive. He just wanted her to live longer.

Liam went to get his younger sister from school. Tamaya was in seventh grade; she was really happy and loved everything about her life. She always came home smiling like she won a prize. Tamaya was the happiest girl he knew. Liam knew she would be heartbroken to know that their mother was gone.

Please send Tamaya Petersons to the front office.

Tamaya leapt up, said goodbye to her classmates in her fourth-period class, grabbed her stuff and started walking down the hallway. When she made it to the front of the building, she knew something was wrong. Liam was crying as much as the teachers were. She almost fell on the floor as she felt fear hit her. "What's going on? Why is everyone crying?" Her older brother stood up and walked over to her slowly, kneeled down and hugged her. She hugged him back, knowing that when he was sad there was a good reason. He finally released her from the embrace and said the worst. "Tamaya, I wish this wasn't true but ... Mom ... is gone."

Tamaya felt as if a wasp stung her heart. *What are we going to do?* was the only thought that went through her mind, over and over again. A whimper escaped her throat before tears started streaming out of her eyes.

When they got home, Liam asked Tamaya, "What do you think about moving in with Dad?" A feeling of rage came rushing back as fast as the day their father had abandoned them. Memories came back from when their mother had just lost her job and Steve, their dad, had decided to leave them. They were left with nothing but bills to pay. So Liam got a job to help while their mom was looking for options. It all ended up with a couple loans and paying back money. Lots of money.

"Are you crazy?" screamed Tamaya. "Remember last time we lived with Dad? He left us! I don't want that to happen again!"

Liam had hoped his younger sister would be okay with it. Until she brought up their dad. He did do terrible things to them, but Liam felt like he had no choice. "Look, I can't pay the bills for the whole house," he explained, "so we have to do something, Tamaya. I have to sell it. I'm only eighteen." It was so confusing to Tamaya; it felt as if it was a nightmare. That night, there wasn't much sleep for the two. Tamaya feared having to live with their dad. Liam got at least five hours of sleep while his younger sister managed seven.

School the next day wasn't easy for Liam. He couldn't stop thinking about his mom in his arms as she died. "Hi, Liam!" His mind cleared when he saw the smiling face of his best friend. "Oh, hey, Anna." She was happy no matter what and magic at making someone's day. Especially Liam's. She had very curly red hair, dark brown eyes and olive skin. Her smile could make anyone feel better. Liam, on the other hand, had dark brown hair, hazel eyes, and pale skin. Then Anna said, "Why do you seem sad? Who did this to you? I will find them and show them what happens when they mess with my best friend!"

Liam sighed and said, "Nobody hurt me."

"It wasn't a joke when you texted that your mom died?"

"No, I'll see you in science. Bye, Anna," Liam said quietly.

Anna was dumbstruck. She went to class and spent the rest of the day in defeat.

All of Tamaya's friends had heard what happened the day before. There was a lot of sympathy. The day was a year long. Tamaya felt uncomfortable and out of place. She missed all of the hugs and kisses that she received every night just before bed. She longed for the heartwarming sound of her mother's voice, the sweet tune of her singing, and the bright-colored clothing she wore every day.

And then the school bell rang. Liam came to grab Tamaya. As they walked home, Tamaya noticed that they took a different turn. She tried to tell Liam, but he insisted that they were going the right way. Soon, they walked up to an apartment complex and all the puzzle pieces came together.

Tamaya screamed at Liam, "Why are we here!? Where is the house? I want Mom back!!" Liam stared at Tamaya, shocked. Tears were streaming down her face as she ran back toward the home they used to live in. She ran as fast as she could away from her older brother. Away from the only person who she could live with. The person who had promised to take care of her. *Lost.* Tamaya was scared. She hid near her school. She hid in her special spot. The spot that she went to when anything bad happened. Tamaya sat there and cried for an hour. She missed home. She missed her mother. It was all messed up.

Tamaya was in her spot for three hours until she heard a soft mumble. "Hello? Who's there?"

She looked around, a little scared of who she might see. When she turned around, Tamaya saw a very tall man behind her.

He had jet black hair with scary green eyes. "I'm David. You can call me Dave." Tamaya curled up and shuffled deeper into her spot without saying a word.

"Hey, no need to be scared. I can help you." Nervous, Tamaya lifted her head and gave him a questioned expression.

"Here, come with me." Dave said calmly. Then Tamaya stood up and followed Dave away from the school.

Tamaya was led to a very small home. The paint was a very faded yellow, and there were a few stains along the top. The steps of the porch were bound to break at any moment. She opened the door, and the inside had a couple chairs and a stained mattress on the ground. "Is this your home?" said Tamaya with a very worried face.

"Yep. This is where I live." Dave smiled at her and asked, "Want something to drink? I have lemonade in the fridge." Seeing the beat-down place made Tamaya wonder what Dave wanted from her. She looked down at her feet while she thought. She politely declined the drink and slowly walked around the house. Her mind wandered off and thought about

Liam and how she had run away furiously. Guilt poured over her like paint. She had finally realized what she had done to him just by running away from him.

"Why do you look sad?" asked Dave.

"I should get going," replied Tamaya. "No no n—" She sprinted toward the door as fast as possible as she figured out she may have fallen into a kidnapper's trap.

Tamaya felt betrayed by the stranger's calm and soothing voice. She ran as fast as possible but was too slow to get away from Dave. He grabbed her arm as it swung back and pulled Tamaya toward him. Scared for her life, she turned her head over and bit him as hard as possible. Dave pulled his hand away, screaming in pain. She dashed away again toward the apartment where she had been just hours earlier. In a panic, she banged on the door as hard as she could, hearing footsteps running up the stairs.

Liam opened the door and Tamaya dashed in and slammed the door closed and locked it before any of them could blink. She immediately pushed Liam and Anna away from the front and went back to it so she could look through the peephole in the door. Just outside of the apartment was Dave. Tamaya held her breath and shushed Liam and Anna just before they spoke.

Then a large fist slammed against the door three times. All of a sudden, Liam grabbed Tamaya and pulled her and Anna into a bedroom and gave them instructions on how they needed to escape. He told them to crawl out the window onto the roof and crawl around to the parking garage. From there, they would need to run down and away to the nearest store. The girls nodded and opened the window to crawl out. Tamaya hugged Liam as hard as possible and turned to shuffle through. The last thing she heard before she turned the corner was a loud crash.

Tamaya turned around to see Liam fall out the window and roll across the rooftop. At the last second, he clutched the edge. In a great struggle, he lifted himself onto the roof again. By this point Anna dragged Tamaya onto the parking garage and picked her up to run down as fast as she could. Running out of energy, Anna put Tamaya down and grabbed her hand. They ran faster than ever before, knowing their lives depended on it.

Liam was running like a squirrel to get away from the guy.

Two weeks had passed since their mother died. The funeral was in an hour. Tamaya and Liam were still haunted by the day of the crash. It had all come back, the emotion, the sadness, and the fear.

During the funeral, Steve, their father, had come up to the stage and said something that his kids would never expect. "She was the love of my life. And I made a terrible mistake. I cheated on her. I left my kids and I was too blind to see that I had abandoned everything I worked so hard for. I'm so very sorry, Liam and Tamaya." He took a sigh and said, "Goodbye, Catherine," and then he left the church.

Hello, my name is Christie. I am thirteen years old and I love writing. I have two dogs, a cat, and a hamster. I live in Colorado with my parents and younger sister since my older sister and brother moved out. I really enjoy playing board games with my family even though they are really good at them and win most of the time. I love to write books with other people because I get to see what they think of the story while they write, so I can change different parts to help the story fit a little better with everything else that is already written. My favorite types of stories to write are mystery, action and thrillers. I usually just write the stories for my entertainment when I get bored. But I hope you enjoyed my short story!

To my family, friends, teachers and fellow classmates for being there/on the phone/or on Zoom and for helping me continue writing. Thank you, Coach Kirsten and Coach Shelly for helping me understand more about writing and how it takes purpose in life. Also, I thank you for helping me so my book would be published. I've been wanting this for a long time, so thank you very much. :)

—Madeline Murray

Doggie and Trumpet Kitty Attack

By
Madeline Murray

CHAPTER 1

"Hello, my name is Sophie. I am going to be your narrator. I have a feeling you will love this book. Sophie, that is me, is going to tell you guys the tale of Doggie and Trumpet. This is Doggie and, of course, she has something to say."

"I need to correct the word 'guys.' There are girls reading this too," said Doggie.

"Sorry about that, folks. Doggie is a little too informative at times," Sophie added.

"I can hear that, Sophie!" said Doggie!

"I hate it when Doggie says that," Sophie sighed.

"I still hear you, Sophie!" said Doggie furiously.

"Okay, I'll stop, but you have to let me finish the story without all these interruptions," said Sophie.

"Okay, Sophie," said Doggie.

"As I was saying, I am about to tell you an epic adventure about when Doggie and Trumpet saved the world," said Sophie. "I know what you're thinking. How can a dog so little save the whole wide world? That's what I thought when I first heard the tale of Doggie and Trumpet," she continued in a calm voice.

"Once upon a time," said Sophie.

"Hey," Mrs. Trumpet called from her seat in the front row. "This story happened two days ago so say, 'Once upon two days ago, there was a dog named Doggie and a president named Trumpet."

"Okay, Mrs. Trumpet," said Sophie in an exasperated way.

"Good, now continue the story, Sophie," said Mrs. Trumpet.

"Before I continue the story, everybody go and say hi to Mrs. Trumpet," said Sophie.

"Hi, Mrs. Trumpet," the children chanted.

"Finally, we can start the story," said Sophie in an annoyed way. "Once upon two days ago, there was a dog named Doggie and a president named Trumpet. Trumpet was on a vacation for two months while Doggie played Mario Brothers for those same two months. When Trumpet got back to the White House, he turned frozen. Kitty Galory was trying to take over the White House," whispered Sophie.

"President Trumpet got the guards and said, 'Off with their heads!'"

"After President Trumpet said that, the Jedas combined their swords and defeated half of Kitty Galory's army," said Sophie."

"Kitty Galory said, 'GET THEM! Don't let them exit the building or I'll water you!'"

"Then Aiden Highwalker came in, making a loud noise," said the narrator.

CHAPTER 2

"Kitty Galory hissed when she heard the noise," said Sophie. "Aiden Highwalker followed the hissing until he found Kitty Galory."

"When Kitty Galory saw Aiden, she said, 'My, oh my, it's the great and powerful cat bully."

"I'm not a cat bully; you are," said Aiden Highwalker.

"You're just saying that 'cause I am a cat," said Kitty Galory.

"Excuse me. This is Trumpet. I'm sorry, but why are you telling the children the scary parts?"

"Oh, sorry, but I have to tell the whole story or it won't be a big hit," said Sophie.

"I don't care, Sophie. That is not okay for the kids," said Trumpet furiously!

"Okay, Mr. Trumpet," said Sophie in surprise.

"Sorry, kids. Everyone interrupts me when I'm the narrator of a story." Sophie sighed. "I should continue before someone interrupts me again."

Grugy interjected, "Hey, no fair. That is what I was about to do. Interrupting is no fun anymore. You know why Doggie,

Trumpet, and I interrupt you."

"I wish that you didn't know why we do it," yelled Grugy.

"Well, it is not my fault, Grugy," sighed Sophie.

Sophie said sadly, "I should continue the story. Instead, here we are, people, in the middle of a war. Hope you enjoy the rest of the story."

Aiden looked over at Kitty Galory and said, "Well, I'm out of ideas. What should we do now?"

"Fight!" said Umil.

"Umil, why did you say that? It's not okay for Jeda students to say that until they are 30 years old," said Aiden in shock.

"I'm not 30 and I'm not Umil," said someone suspiciously.

Aiden said, "Who are you then?"

"Aiden Highwalker, my name is Belto."

"What, that is crazy, but where is Umil?" asked Aiden Highwalker worriedly?

"Umil is inside her cave with her husband," said Belto.

CHAPTER 3

"Belto, why are you here?" inquired Aiden.

"I'm here because, well ... you're all in danger," Belto warned. "The kitties you are fighting now are just robots. Kitty Galory's real army is coming very soon. There is no time to waste!"

"That is right, Aiden. I'm just a robot made to look like someone that is not me," said the pretend Kitty Galory.

"Aiden, use the water in this bucket to water the pretend

Kitty Galory," said Belto breathlessly. "Hurry, before it attacks you."

"Okay, Belto," said Aiden. "Let's do this thing!"

"Aiden, join me. We can rule the world together," said the pretend Kitty Galory.

"No way, Jose. I'm not ever going to turn on your side," said Aiden.

"Will you at least not water me?" begged the imitation Kitty Galory.

"Sorry, Kitty Brat, no way," Aiden snarked at her.

"Well, the robot Kitty Galory is finished. I see that all the other kitty robots have been finished off too. Thank you, Belto, for warning me about that. Now I must destroy Kitty Galory and her army's headquarters before they exit it."

"Bye, Belto!" said Aiden.

"Bye, Aiden!" Belto answered loudly.

"While Aiden was heading to Kitty Galory's headquarters, Belto was telling Grugy and Umil to find shelter and filling them in on what was happening," said the narrator. "It is a long way to Kitty Galory's headquarters, so Aiden asked Queen Amelia and her unicorn, Lady Lovely, to help. The two girls agreed. Aiden gave Queen Amelia a weapon to help fight. Then they continued their travel."

"Meanwhile, Belto wasn't having a good time," said the narrator. "Umil was freaking out."

"Umil said she wanted Grugy to move with her to a place a long way from their cave," said the narrator.

"No way, Umil," said Belto.

CHAPTER 4

"They got eyes everywhere," said Belto. "They can see a kilometer with their gear."

"Do not look outside of the cave," Belto warned.

"How did you know that I was going to ask that question?" asked Umil.

"Umil, Belto never tells anybody his personal answers," said Belto.

"Man, I really want to know how you do it," said Umil.

"I hope that Umil can deal with all that is going on until the war is over," said Belto.

"Yeah, I hope so too, Belto," said Grugy.

"I'm glad you're not freaking out about this, Grugy," said Belto.

"It's no big deal. This cave keeps me and my wife safe no matter what problem we're in; that is why I'm not freaking out, Belto," said Grugy.

"Okay, Grugy. Bye-bye," said Belto.

"Bye, Belto," said Grugy.

"Bye," said Umil.

"Okay, you two, stay inside and stay safe," said Belto.

"Remember, do not look outside," said Belto.

"Okay, Belto," said Grugy and Umil in unison.

"Let us get back to Aiden, Queen Amelia, and Lady Lovely," said the narrator. "They have already finished half of their trip, but right now they're getting water."

"While they were getting their water, two robots came up behind them," said Sophie, the narrator.

"Then Amelia saw that it was B2-D2 and B-3po," Sophie added.

Then Amelia said, "Hi, B2-D2 and B-3po."

Then B2-D2 and B-3po replied, "Hi, Aiden. Hi, Queen Amelia, and hi, Lady Lovely."

"We're glad that you all are safe," the three responded in unison.

"Us too," said B2-D2 and B-3po.

"The family is back together, everyone," said B2-D2.

"You are so right, B2-D2. Time to head South-East," Queen Amelia said. "It's faster that way and has perfect weather now."

"I agree with Amelia," added Aiden.

"Thank you, Aiden. Do the rest of you agree with me?" asked Amelia.

"Yep," said Lady Lovely.

"Yep," said B2-D2.

"Yep," said B-3po.

"Then," Amelia said, "Good. All of you agree. Now let's get back on the trail."

CHAPTER 5

"So where have you been all this time?" asked Aiden.

"We have been captured by Kitty Galory's army," said B2-D2. "Then we got saved by Guyo himself."

"B2-D2, how is that possible?" Aiden asked in surprise. "We thought Guyo said he was heading North-West not South-East."

"Guyo said to not tell you until he comes back from his journey," said B2-D2.

"My, that is a bummer, right, Aiden?" asked Amelia.

"Okay, okay, yah, yah," said Aiden.

"Aiden, are you listening to me or not?" asked Amelia.

"Oh sorry, Amelia. I was distracted by this tag here, said Aiden.

Amelia said to Aiden, "This is the last part of the map, and there is a clue on the back of it. It says that it is from Guyo and to use it for our journey."

"Everybody stop their camels and listen up," shouted Queen Amelia. "This is how we'll sneak into Kitty Galory's headquarters. First, we'll knock out two knights and get into their clothes. Then we'll act like we caught prisoners."

She then said, "B2-D2 and B-3po are going to be the prisoners. Aiden and I are going to turn you two in. Does everybody get the first part of the plan?" she asked.

"Yes, Queen Amelia, yes, we do," B2-D2, B-3po, and Aiden answered in a rush.

"Good, we will talk about the next part of the plan later, but now we have to hurry," said Amelia.

"Hello, this is your narrator. We're having a little trouble with the idea robot, so we can't continue the story until I fix it. I will have to find you something else to do. What about knock-knock jokes? Hmm ... nope, that won't do."

"One second, children ... sorry about that, there was a mistake. The idea robot actually was having a glitch, so don't worry and sit back and enjoy reading the rest of the story. Start at Queen Amelia was saying they had to hurry. After two hours Aiden, Queen Amelia, B2-D2, and

B-3po got to Kitty Galory's headquarters," said Sophie.

CHAPTER 6

"So this is the second part of our plan. As soon as we get inside the building, we will head toward the prison," said Amelia. "After that we will put a cell opener on each cell and set it for twenty-five minutes. That should give us enough time to sneak past the other guards, get to the control room, maybe fight Kitty Galory and turn on the shutdown button, which also makes it explode."

"Also it will give you robots, B2-D2 and B-3po, and the other prisoners enough time to exit the building. Everybody get the second part of the plan?" asked Amelia.

"Yep, we do," said Aiden, B2-D2 and B-3po.

"Okay everybody, let's go," said Amelia.

"Hello, guards, we are turning in these two robots that got out of headquarters, so we need to get in," said Aiden.

"Here you go," said the guard.

"The team of heroes made it inside the building, but they still have to shut down Kitty Galory's headquarters. Let's see if our heroes can do it," said the narrator in a mysterious voice. "After five minutes they got to the prison. Then Aiden and Queen Amelia put a cell opener on each cell and set the timer for twenty-five minutes. Before they did that, they put B2-D2 and B-3po in a cell."

"Then they headed toward the control room. After five minutes they reached the control room. All of a sudden, Aiden and Queen Amelia heard a noise," the narrator said excitedly. "Then Kitty Galory came into the room and said, sarcastically, 'Hello, Aiden. Hello, Queen Amelia. It's nice to see you on such a beautiful day.'"

"Sorry, but we're not Aiden and Queen Amelia; we're just holograms," said the disguised Aiden and Queen Amelia. "The real Aiden and Amelia are behind you, Kitty Galory," said the pretend Aiden and Queen Amelia.

"Hello, Kitty Galory, you were tricked by your worst enemies, me and Queen Amelia," said Aiden.

"Well, is that so? said Kitty Galory, sarcastically again. "Let's fight to prove it."

"Okay," replied Aiden and Amelia just as sarcastically. "If you say so."

CHAPTER 7

"After five minutes Kitty Galory's back legs started to hurt," said the narrator. "That is because Kitty Galory hadn't been doing her karate lately. Aiden and Queen Amelia were in pain too, but that didn't stop them. Suddenly Guyo came into the room and helped Aiden and Queen Amelia finish off Kitty Galory."

"They had more to do though. Two minutes later Aiden, Queen Amelia, and Guyo got to the spot where Kitty Galory put the shutdown button. After that, they shut down Kitty Galory's headquarters. Next, Aiden, Queen Amelia, and Guyo helped everyone exit the building. All of a sudden, Queen Amelia saw a girl who was hurt and needed help," said the narrator in a surprised way.

"Then Queen Amelia said, 'There is a girl in there. I need to help her.'

"Aiden said, 'No, it's too dangerous.' But it was too late."

"Amelia rushed into the building to save the little girl," said the narrator.

"Everyone thought Queen Amelia and the little girl were goners," said Sophie sadly. "Later Aiden saw a face and said they made it."

"Aiden is right; they did make it," said Sophie. "Everybody partied all night long, then they headed home in the morning."

"Hello, this is your narrator speaking even more and more. Before I end the story, I'd like to tell you who Aiden and Queen Amelia really are. Aiden Highwalker is Trumpet and Queen Amelia is Doggie and Mrs. Trumpet."

"Did you guys and girls like the book? If you do, I'm really happy. I'm glad that it is almost time to go home. I wish I could spend some more time with you, but I can't. I can't wait to see what happens on our heroes' next adventure with you. I hope you can't either."

"I've got to go now. Bye."

Madeline is an author, artist, musician and
fourth-grader. She is interested in becoming an
author one day. Madeline loves birds, horses
and food. She started writing stories at nine.
Madeline lives in Cotopaxi, Colorado,
with her family and her pets.

This story is for the best baby brother in the world, Julesie, and the silliest sister in the world, Teddy. I love you both.

—Brooks Lopez

From the Stars

By
Brooks Lopez

PROLOGUE

Lately, I have had trouble with the school bully, and normally I would ask my grandmother for advice, but she's far away. I miss my grandmother because she's on Earth. I decided to write a postcard in the mail. They're old-school, but there's no way of it getting intercepted because no one will think to do it.

Dear Grandma,
   I miss you here on Mars. Right now, I'm hanging out with friends. I'm having some trouble with the school bully. Do you have any suggestions? Please write back as soon as possible.

With love,
Josh

CHAPTER 1

"Does anyone have a strange feeling?" I asked." No, that's just you," answered Saffron Dalton, my best friend. Or one of them. The others are Sol Mathews and Brianna "Bri" Moore. I'm Joshua Amor, but my friends call me Josh. As we walked into school, we ran into the school bully, Dominique Savage. He shoved us, knocking me into Saffron, creating a domino effect. Dominique was laughing, as I muttered, "He is savage."

Thankfully, he didn't hear me. He seems to have super hearing. All Martians do. We live in a bustling colony on Mars. We have to wear spacesuits outside, but inside, we're fine. They aren't very bulky, but it's still impossible to shake hands with the gloves on. Around buildings there are bubbles. Anyway, I hate having Dominique at school. He's been the bully since kindergarten. And it hasn't gotten any better; it's gotten worse. He went from breaking crayons to breaking bones. The weird feeling came back, only worse this time. Like something was *wrong*. I decided to ignore it for the rest of the day.

"Hey, do you guys want to come to my place today?" Sol asked. We all agreed. As we put our spacesuits on, I couldn't help but wonder, *What is wrong?* When we got there, I told them about the feeling. They said they now felt it too.

Sol said, "It also seems to get worse when Dominique is near."

I agreed, "Yeah, like it's him."

"Let's investigate," suggested Bri.

"Okay, but we don't even know where he lives," I said.

"I have an idea," added Saffron slyly.

The next day, after school, we put our plan into action.

After the bell rings, we follow Dominique, but we hide behind things along the way. If he discovers we are following him, and he runs, we chase him. Then we investigate his house. If he has anything weird, we'll find it. As we follow him, he doesn't notice us. He walks into his house, and I write the address down in my notebook. We decide to divide and conquer. Then we will report back our findings. When I sneak around, I find a bulletin board, but it seems evil. I see what looks like a giant satellite dish, like a death ray. And the Earth, but that's all I see because I see Dominique coming, so I have to get out.

When we meet up, Saffron says she found giant pieces of metal. I follow up to that with my answer, the bulletin board."

They must somehow be connected," says Sol.

"Oh no, Dominique is building a death ray to destroy the Earth," says Saffron, frantically.

"Then we have to stop him," I answer, bravely and boldly. "Tomorrow, we—oh, wait, never mind." I do a double-take.

"What were you going to say?" asks Bri.

"I was going to say, 'tomorrow we confront him,' but we will each get beaten to a pulp," I say.

"I don't care. We should just do it," says Sol.

After school the next day, which is a Friday, we all go to Dominique's locker. He's still there.

"We know you're trying to destroy the Earth," Sol says assertively.

Wh-whadya mean?" he stutters.

"We got into your house," I say flatly.

"Oh," he says, then runs. I start running after him. He's got a fifteen-step lead, but I run track. He's stumbling over his own feet. But it's hard to catch up to him because he has giant strides. He bursts out the doors, but runs into the plexiglass of the bubble, forgetting all about it. I step on top of him. He grabs my foot. I know what's coming, but it comes too fast to react. He flips me on my head. Then he beats me up, as I anticipated. I leave with a bloody nose, a broken tooth, and many bruises. He could have done way worse. But now I have to explain to my mom what happened. And a dentist has to shove my tooth back in my mouth. That's when my friends come.

"Aaareeee yoo okkay?" Oh, and a concussion.

"No," I reply. They help me get up. The pain I'm in is immense. We walk over to the nurse with the support of Saffron and Sol. She confirms the concussion, and she also says that I don't have a broken nose. She wants me to visit a real doctor. They help me walk home. And talk for me, because my mouth is full of blood.

"He got beaten up by the bully," says Sol, flatly.

"You have got to stop engaging with that boy," says my mom.

"He didn't; he just came at him," Saffron says. "Anyway, he has a concussion. The nurse recommended a doctor."

"Okay," sighs my mom.

After I'm all fixed up, I call my friends. It's a Saturday, so we can't meet at school. We meet at Sol's house and go into his room in the basement.

"We know Dominique is building a death ray. How do we stop him?" I ask." I say we stop him by force," says Sol.

"Me too," says Saffron, which surprises me. We take a vote on it, and it's unanimous. On Monday, after school, we tell every kid we know. We say that on Friday, they all go to this Dominique's address and overpower him. And tell them to pass it on to every kid they know.

CHAPTER 2

Friday, the big day. Finally. The bell rings—*rrriiinnnggg*. Half the student body waits eagerly. They all walk home, but that's part of the plan. In about twenty minutes, Saffron, Sol, Bri, and I will walk down the middle of the street. The people who were told will join.

Then my phone alarm goes off. We nod to each other. Then we march. All the kids on the street join. Then the neighborhood. Then the entire sixth-grade student body. Except for Dominique. Then we reach his house. The rest is history.

EPILOGUE

Dominique is now on Earth, serving time, picking up trash and dog poop. All for free. School is more fun now. We got extra credit in history class for our "peaceful protest." All is well with the universe again.

Brooks Lopez was born and raised in Colorado. He is ten years old and loves playing baseball, reading, all things space, and creative writing. He lives with his mom, dad, seven-year-old sister Teddy, eighteen-month-old brother Jules, and giant golden retriever Leo. Brooks will be in the fifth grade, and he wants to be a scientist when he grows up.

Tween Camp and Anthology Acknowledgments

Thank you to award-winning author Nancy Oswald for kicking off camp and guiding the campers through fun, interactive games and writing exercises. You set the stage and a wonderful tone for camp.

Thank you to award-winning author and editor Catherine Spader for sharing your insights on show don't tell with fun picture prompts at camp!

To award-winning author Marcia Canter, thank you for being a camp counselor for a day and sharing about character development. Our campers enjoyed having their characters write postcards to each other.

To top-notch editor and camp counselor Angela Renkoski, thank you for insights on metaphors. Our campers found you so inspiring! Thank you for generously proofreading for the anthology, as well!

To Sandra Arellano, of Denver Pain & Performance Solutions, thank you for donating to our scholarships to support our campers. You have a kind heart and a wonderful pilates studio.

To Polly Letofsky, My Word Publishing founder and award-winning author, thank you for helping guide and brainstorm the curriculum and program. You are a wonderful mentor.

To Victoria Wolf, our favorite cover and interior designer in the world. Thank you for teaching the campers about cover and interior design and for your work on this anthology. You are a rock star!

To Coach Shelly Wilhelm, thank you for teaching these writers about hooks and opening lines, as well as your office hours with campers, and your editing. You truly made this an unforgettable experience for campers, challenging them to write the best stories they could. We could not have done this program without you.

To Coach Kirsten Jensen, thank you so much for having the idea for a writing camp and bringing together these talented writers and mentors. It was an absolute highlight of my summer. I had the joy of working individually with each camper and seeing their faces light up when we talked about writing techniques and editing. You showed me how distance camp could be so successful. You are the best!

To our authors,

All eight of you are gifted and brilliant writers. We were lucky to have had such an amazing group for our first tween writing camp and anthology. Thank you for showing up and working hard. We appreciated all of you for being so dedicated, asking questions, sharing, learning and revising. We learned from you too.

To Monte, your humor and big, bright ideas amazed us.

To Riley, you were already such a great writer, and it was so fun to see your skills grow.

To Ellyse, you have a deep and beautiful world of imagination within. Thanks for sharing it with us.

To Helena, we truly love your sense of humor and creativity.

To Madeline, we enjoyed your passion for stories, and that you take risks and try cool things with your writing.

To Brooks, you are an amazing writer and a dedicated baseball player!

To Anika, you are intense and deep, a fearless writer.

To Christie, you are not just a wonderful and serious writer, but a great leader.

Thank you campers for making our summer so much brighter.

Readers, we invite you to tell us what you're feeling on the following pages or write your own story.

Now It's Your
Turn to write